W9-BEA-563

STRANGE CREATURES

PAULINE CARTWRIGHT

ILLUSTRATED BY LORENZO VAN DER LINGEN

Learning Media

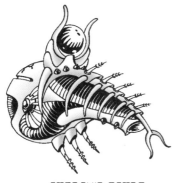

STARSHIP ASTRA

SHUTTLE 2

After their adventure with the Andrals, the crew of the starship ASTRA traveled at light speed to the Terron star system to look for new planets. They went into orbit around a blue planet that looked a lot like Earth. Zimm and Tarek were sent down in their shuttle for a closer look.

ZIMM

TAREK

1

OUT OF CONTROL

"Shuttle to *Astra* command. We are ready to leave for the surface," said Tarek.

"Keep in touch," replied Captain Voss. "Remember the trouble we had the last time your radio failed."

"We'll never forget our adventure with the Andrals," said Zimm. "Don't worry. We'll keep our eyes open." Zimm and Tarek were excited about exploring this new world. The sensors on the *Astra* had shown that there was something unusual living there.

As the shuttle sped away from the starship, Tarek loaded a scanner to send down to the planet. "This will tell us more about what is living on the surface. From here, it looks a lot like your home world," he said.

"Yes, I hope it's safe," said Zimm. "I haven't been back to Earth for so long. It would be nice to see green grass and blue water."

"I would rather swim in the red seas on my planet," said Tarek. "Blue water always looks strange to me."

Zimm and Tarek were pleased to be exploring together again. They began talking about the other adventures they had shared. Suddenly there was a loud crash, and the shuttle shook. Zimm's hands slipped from the controls. "What's happening?" she cried.

"Meteors!" said Tarek. "Put up the shields."

"It's too late," said Zimm. "We've lost power. The controls have gone crazy!"

They felt another huge crash against the side of the shuttle, and then a lot of thumps as the smaller meteors hit them. The shuttle shook this way and that. Then, all at once, it went into a spin. It turned over and over, out of control.

"Come in, *Astra*!" called Zimm. "We're in trouble! Come in, Captain!"

"We have lost contact with *Astra*," said Tarek. "We are on our own."

The shuttle began falling fast toward the surface of the planet. "Warning! Warning!" sounded the computer. "Prepare for crash-landing!"

2

WHERE ARE WE?

Tarek opened his eyes. He moved his head … his arms … his legs. He looked around. Zimm was there beside him, still safe in her seat. She was looking at the sky through a large, jagged hole in the side of their ship. The shuttle had flipped onto its side in the crash. "It's cracked open like an egg," she said.

"It looks bad," said Tarek. "We will need help to fix it."

Suddenly Zimm shouted, "Look! Look outside!"

Tarek turned to the window. He expected to see something dangerous coming toward them. Instead he saw flowers – beautiful flowers in bright colors with yellow and silver centers. They had crash-landed beside a forest of flowers. They had never seen anything like it.

They tried to call the *Astra,* but the radio and the computer were not working. They climbed out of the smashed shuttle.

"At least we're not hurt," said Zimm, "and we can breathe. It *is* like Earth."

Tarek looked at the hole in the shuttle. "Yes! There must be oxygen here, or we would have been dead by now," he said. He took a radio alarm from his pack and put it on the ground.

3

DON'T TOUCH

"All we can do now is wait," said Zimm.

"The radio alarm should tell the *Astra* exactly where we are," said Tarek. "I hope they come soon."

"If we're here for a long time, we'll have to look for food," said Zimm. "We might have to eat these," she laughed, pointing at the flowers. She reached out to a red flower with a fluffy center.

"Stop!" cried Tarek. "Remember the rule! Never touch plants or creatures until we have scanned them." He pulled Zimm's hand away from the plant, but it was too late. There was a shower of yellow pollen. It fell on Tarek's hand and face. He cried out in pain and fell to the ground.

Zimm ran to the shuttle to get the medical kit. When she got back, Tarek was sitting up. He was looking at his hand. It had a red rash all over it. Zimm looked at Tarek's face. The rash was there too. "Help me!" he cried. He fell back again and started to moan in pain.

Zimm tried to think. What was happening? Tarek had been poisoned. She was scared to touch him in case she became poisoned too.

Suddenly Tarek started scratching at his face and hands. He tried to tear off his clothes and shoes. "No, Tarek," cried Zimm, "you need your clothes to protect you."

"Help me, Zimm," Tarek whispered. Then he passed out.

Zimm pulled a blanket from the kit. She rolled Tarek onto it with her feet and carefully wrapped it around him. She searched on her power pad for ways that she could help Tarek. There was nothing there.

Zimm felt very frightened. The shuttle was smashed, they couldn't call the *Astra*, Tarek was very ill … she had to do something! She dragged her friend back to the shuttle. Then she ran off down a pathway between the flowers.

4

EYES WATCHING

Zimm came to a small pool. Water! Maybe that would help. She scanned the pool to find out if the water was OK to drink. Then she bent down to fill up a bottle. She felt as if eyes were watching her. Was there someone or something close by?

On the way back to the shuttle, she carried her freeze-beam in one hand and the water in the other. She looked around carefully, but she couldn't see anything.

Zimm splashed the water onto Tarek's rash, but it didn't help. He was still in pain. Zimm felt more worried than ever. The radio alarm was sending out a signal, but there was no sign of help. Had the *Astra* been caught in the meteor shower too? Maybe no help would come!

Zimm was hungry, but she didn't dare to touch any plants. She drank the water and tried to give some to Tarek. She still felt as if someone was watching her. She needed to rest. She lay down by Tarek, but it took her hours to get to sleep.

In the night, she woke suddenly and jumped to her feet. Something was wrong. Tarek was gone! Then she saw him. He had been moved close to a muddy bank. All around him were strange little creatures.

5

MIND TALK

The creatures were very small. They only reached up to Zimm's knee. They had round bodies covered with brown fur. Their arms and legs were covered with skin like leather. All that Zimm could see on each face was a nose and two large, brown eyes. Those were the eyes that had watched her!

The creatures were taking yellow mud from a hole in the bank and putting it on Tarek. Whatever were they doing to him? She held her freeze-beam in front of her. She walked toward Tarek and the strange creatures. Suddenly, inside her head, she heard voices. "We are helping your friend. Do not harm us."

Zimm stopped, amazed. The creatures without mouths were talking to her mind! She walked closer. Tarek looked up and said, "Do not worry, Zimm. These creatures *do* talk to your mind. They have made me feel much better – this mud is very soothing. They say to leave it on until morning."

Tarek's hand and face were covered with the yellow mud. The creatures picked up the blanket and carried him back to the shuttle. In her mind, Zimm heard the creatures say, "Wash the mud off in the morning. Then he will be well."

"Thank you!" she called. "Thank you!" The creatures were disappearing back into the flower forest. Zimm knew that she and Tarek needed more help. She didn't want them to go. Where would they find food?

"You will be all right," Zimm heard the creatures saying in her head. "You won't need food." They knew what she was thinking.

Zimm and Tarek sat staring into the flower forest. All the furry, brown creatures had gone.

6

BACK HOME

Just as it was getting light, Zimm and Tarek heard a sound above them. They could see the lights of the rescue shuttle. The *Astra* had heard their signal!

"And the creatures knew before we did," thought Zimm. "That's why they told me not to worry."

Back on the starship *Astra*, Captain Voss said, "The meteor shower hit us too. We had to make some repairs."

Zimm told Captain Voss about the crash and the forest of flowers. She told him about Tarek being ill and about the strange creatures. But Tarek didn't say how he had got the pollen on his skin.

"I'd like to know how the mud helped you, Tarek," said Captain Voss, "and I'd like to meet the creatures that can talk with their minds."

"Perhaps we should go back?" asked Tarek. "There is a lot to learn on this planet. And this time we will remember the rules." He looked at Zimm.

Captain Voss looked surprised. "What rules?"

"All the rules," said Zimm quickly. "All starship rules are important on an unknown planet."

Later, Tarek teased Zimm. "Captain Voss might come back with us. The furry creatures could teach him how to talk and listen with his mind. Then what will you do?"

"He can listen to my mind if he wants to," said Zimm. "When we go back, I'll be remembering every rule there is."